Louisa and Phoebe
by Adèle Geras

A Red Fox Book

Published by Random House Children's Books
20 Vauxhall Bridge Road, London SW1V 2SA

A division of Random House UK Ltd
London Melbourne Sydney Auckland
Johannesburg and agencies throughout the world

1 3 5 7 9 10 8 6 4 2

First published in Great Britain by Red Fox 1997

Printed and bound in Great Britain by Cox & Wyman Ltd, Reading, Berks

Papers used by Random House UK Limited are natural, recyclable products made from
wood grown in sustainable forests. The manufacturing processes conform to the
environmental regulations of the country of origin.

RANDOM HOUSE UK Limited Reg. No. 954009

ISBN 0 09 921852 6

For Joanna Carey

LITTLE SWAN BALLET BOOKS
1 Little Swan
2 Louisa's Secret
3 Louisa in the Wings
4 Louisa and Phoebe

Little Swan

BOOK 4

Louisa and Phoebe

by Adèle Geras

illustrated by Karen Popham

Red Fox

·······Chapter One·······

Saturday is usually my best day of the whole week, because that's when I go to my special ballet class. I started going in the spring. Miss Matting spoke to Mum, and Mum phoned Dad. I made Mum tell me what Miss Matting had said to her.

"She said you had a gift for ballet, Weezer, and she wants you to go to her advanced class on Saturday mornings. Dad and I have agreed that you should."

That was one of the happiest days of my whole life, and I didn't even mind Mum calling me Weezer because I liked what she was saying so much.

There were ten of us in the special class. Then, a couple of months after I started, Miss Matting said she thought Tony should come too, so now we go together. It's very useful having him living next door. It means that we can both go over all the steps and routines, which makes them more fun. I don't mind a bit when Tony tells me what's wrong with something I'm doing, which is funny, because usually I hate being criticized. Miss Matting told me off about it once.

"Louisa," she said, "the greater your talent, the more critical I have to be. You do realize that, don't you?"

"Yes, Miss Matting," I said.

"Then we won't have you pulling sulky faces ever again, will we?"

"No, Miss Matting," I said. Was it possible that all the really great ballerinas never sulked? I didn't think so, not really. Still, I made up my mind to sulk less, and to keep my sulking hidden from Miss Matting if I ever felt like doing it during a class.

After that I was very good and well-behaved for ages, until today. I didn't exactly sulk today, but I was annoyed, and I kept on being annoyed even after I got home. My sister Annie noticed at once.

"What's the matter with you?" she asked.

"Nothing," I mumbled.

"Then why have you just thrown your precious ballet suitcase across the room like that?"

I flopped on to my bed and spoke into the pillow.

"I can't hear a word you're saying," Annie said at last. "Sit up and talk to me properly."

I did sit up in the end. "A new girl came to Miss Matting's today. She's come from another ballet class, on the other side of town, because everyone knows that our class is so good."

"Is that a reason for you to be so grumpy?"

"I am *not* grumpy!" I said. "I'm just annoyed."

"But why?"

"I told you. It's because of this new girl."

"What's the matter with her? Does she bite? Did she kick you? I don't understand, Weezer."

"LOUISA!" I hissed. Annie never seemed to learn. I wanted to be called by my proper name. A real Russian ballet dancer had told me it was romantic.

"Louisa," said Annie. "Sorry. Tell me about this girl. Is she ugly?"

"No, she's pretty. She has lovely brown hair with reddish bits in it. Not carroty red, but beautiful dark red."

"Where does she go to school?"

"Somewhere fancy, I expect. Her voice is dead posh. And you should see her car. It's huge, and it's so clean it shines."

"Your voice is quite posh," said Annie.

"Quite posh isn't the same as dead posh. She also says silly things in the changing-room, like 'oh my golly' and 'cripes'. Can you imagine any normal person saying 'cripes'?"

"Well, I wouldn't say it and you wouldn't, but it doesn't seem like a very good reason to dislike a person."

"That isn't why I dislike her," I said. "Though it doesn't make me like her any better."

"What is it then?"

"She's got a silly name."

"Tell me," said Annie.

"She's called Phoebe."

"I think that's a beautiful name."

"You don't! Not really. You can't . . . you just can't. It's a pathetic name."

"It's not pathetic. It's just old-fashioned," Annie said.

"Well, then it suits her. *She's* old-fashioned."

"How do you know?"

"I can tell," I said. "She was wearing a horrible pleated skirt. And shiny shoes. No one wears shoes like that any more. They're too babyish. We all wear trainers."

"That's still no reason not to like her. If you only liked people because of what they wore, then you wouldn't have any friends."

Annie is such a creep! I could feel myself getting cross with *her* now so I said, "I don't want to talk about it any more. It's boring. Talk about something else, Annie, for goodness' sake."

We went downstairs for supper and I forgot about Phoebe for a while. I remembered her again as I was trying to get to sleep. I thought about what I'd said to Annie. I hadn't told her the real reason I was annoyed. I didn't want to admit it, even to myself. It was because the new girl was a good dancer. She was definitely as good as I was, and in the dark it was easier to think something that made me feel really bad: maybe she was even better. I know you aren't supposed to mind about things like that, but I did. I just couldn't help it. I wish, I said to myself, I wish, wish, wish, that she would find another class to go to somewhere else. I wish she'd just disappear.

·······Chapter Two·······

Phoebe didn't disappear. She came to the Saturday ballet class every week, and everyone else seemed to like her. She always chatted away as we got changed, and Eleanor and Michelle hung around her all the time. They said things like, "Oh, Phoebe, I really love your hairband!" or, "Where did you get that leotard?"

And she'd try to tell them, only she wasn't really much use because she'd say, "Gosh, I can't remember. I think my mother got it for me," or, "I honestly don't know."

I didn't mind other people being friends with her. I had best friends of my own: Tricia and Maisie, who didn't come to the Saturday class. I also had Tony to go and come back with, but all the same, Eleanor and Michelle and I used to be a kind of threesome. I suppose we could have become a foursome, but I still didn't like Phoebe. She was always nice to me and this made me feel even worse. She wasn't a bit shy. If there was something she wanted to say, she just came right over to you and said it.

Also, she often asked me to show her things. One day she said, "Louisa, I really like the way you do pirouettes. Will you help me with mine?" So I showed her how I did them, and she copied me, and I corrected the way she was holding her arms, and after a while her pirouettes *were* looking much smoother.

"Thanks tons, Louisa," she said. That was a typically Phoebe-ish thing to say. No one else would ever use an expression like that. She smiled at me.

"I'm breathless now, and a bit dizzy. I'll never do them like you, of course, but I feel much happier with them now. You're a fantastically lively, sparkly kind of dancer. I'll never be as good as you."

I couldn't believe my ears. Did Phoebe *really* think I was 'fantastically lively and sparkly', or was she just saying so to try and get me to be a little more friendly? I liked her a bit better just for saying such a nice thing, and I knew I should have said something nice back to her, but I didn't. I just smiled and said, "Thanks, Phoebe."

I could hear Annie's voice in my head, saying, "Go on, Weezer, be a bit more friendly. It won't hurt you," but I didn't feel like being friendly, and I was a little ashamed of myself as I watched Phoebe walk over to the barre.

At the end of the class, Miss Matting said, "Go and change as quickly as possible, please, and then come and sit in here. I have some very exciting news for you all."

In the changing room everyone was giggling, wondering what the news would be.

"They want some kids for an advert," said Michelle.

"They're making a movie and need us for extras." That was Debbie.

"I bet it's a documentary about ballet schools," said Emma.

I didn't bother to wonder, but got changed as quickly as I could. We all did. Miss Matting laughed when she saw the whole class sitting quietly, waiting.

"Well," she said, "now I know how to get you all to hurry. I shall dangle exciting bits of news in front of you. But what I have to tell you now really *is* special. You've heard of the Sheridan Ballet Company, haven't you?"

We all nodded. The Sheridan was our local company.

"As you know, they always put on *The Nutcracker* at the Theatre Royal for the two weeks before Christmas, and with this particular ballet, they choose children from dance schools in the area to be in the production. Now I'm sure you're all familiar with *The Nutcracker* but for anyone who isn't, it has several parts for children. Dominic Sheridan himself is coming here next week to audition you all. He's looking for a dozen young dancers to be mice, I think, and four to be party guests and double up as children in the Land of Sweets in Act Two. You must remember, though, that other schools in the area are also being auditioned, so it's quite possible that none of you will be chosen. You must all be perfectly clear about that. Are you quite clear, Louisa dear?"

"Yes, Miss Matting," I said. Why did she ask me specially? I would have to talk to Tony about it on the way home. I couldn't wait to tell Annie. *The Nutcracker* was the very first ballet I ever saw and I'd watched the video hundreds of times. I must be chosen, I said to myself as we all stood up and made our way out of the hall. I must, must, must be chosen. Phoebe was right beside me as we left.

"I bet Mr Sheridan chooses you," she said to me, and she was actually smiling as she said it, almost as though she wouldn't have minded at all.

"No," I said, "I bet he chooses you," and I managed to smile as well. I even managed to say something nice. I said, "I think you really deserve to be chosen."

Annie would have been proud of me. I was proud of myself, and felt good all the way home, even though I was still anxious. How would I get through the next week, till the audition?

"I'm going to watch my *Nutcracker* video tonight," I told Tony. "Come and watch it too, if you like. Then we can see what we're going to be asked to do."

"Great!" said Tony. "Thanks."

He looked as though he couldn't care less about the audition. I didn't understand how anyone could be so easy-going.

·····Chapter Three·····

I spent most of the next week when I wasn't in school or in bed practising for the audition. Annie and Mum got quite sick of me pretending to be a mouse.

"Stop nibbling your toast like that," Mum said. "You look ridiculous."

"She's still being a mouse," Annie explained.

"I know she's being a mouse, but I don't remember any toast-nibbling scenes in *Nutcracker*," said Mum. "I think all the mice do is have a fight, and rush around the stage waving swords, and swishing their tails about. The King Mouse has a slipper thrown at him. I do remember that."

"I'm being in character," I explained. My mum doesn't understand about character. "If you're a mouse, then everything you do has to be mouse-like."

"Doesn't this Mr Sheridan want some nice, well-behaved children to go to a Christmas party at the beginning of Act One?" Annie asked. "You could practise being a well-behaved child."

"I'll never be chosen as one of those," I said. "My only chance is to be the best and most mouse-like mouse in the world. Phoebe will probably be a party child . . . it would suit her. She always looks as if she's just off to some posh do or other."

"Well, just for now," said Mum, "please sit normally on your chair and eat your breakfast like a human being."

"I'm glad I don't have to walk to school with you any more," Annie said. She had started going to Fairvale High in September, so now I walked to school with Tony.

"That's not a very nice thing to say," said Mum. "Poor old Weezer, she's not that bad, is she?"

"Not usually," said Annie, "only I saw her and Tony going off yesterday, and they looked really mad. What were you doing, Weezer?"

"Louisa," I said. "We were scampering. Mice scamper, in case you didn't know."

"I think," said Annie, "that we should call you 'Cheezer' from now on."

I threw my piece of toast at her, and it missed her and hit poor Brad, our cat, who was curled up on the kitchen chair.

"Stop it, girls," said Mum. "Go and get ready for school, both of you. I don't want any more of this silly mouse nonsense. Goodness knows what will happen if you *do* get the part, Louisa. We'll have to put up with you being a full-time mouse."

"It's OK," I said. "There's not much chance, really. Miss Matting said so." But even as I said it, I was crossing my fingers under the table, just for luck.

There was about half an hour after I got back from school before Annie arrived. Usually, I went to Tony's house, but today I decided to go and visit Mrs Posnansky. She is always a good person to talk to if you are worried. She never laughs at me, and she never thinks I am silly to care so much about ballet. That is because her mother was a real ballerina, years and years ago, and Mrs Posnansky truly believed me when I said I was going to be a ballet dancer too. I like her house. It is dark and quiet and she always gives her guests lovely cakes and biscuits.

"Come, Little Swan," she said when she saw me at the door. "Is tomorrow the big audition? You must be nervous. Come and eat and drink and you will feel better."

I don't mind Mrs Posnansky calling me Little Swan. In my extra-special treasures box, I keep the headdress her mother wore when she was in *Swan Lake* and which she gave me for my first dancing display.

"Now tell everything," she said, as I drank my tea and ate a brandy snap. "Is a mouse you wish to be? In *The Nutcracker?*"

"I don't mind what I am," I said, and in a way it was true. "Imagine! We'd be in a real theatre, performing for two weeks. We'd be with all the grown-up dancers. Would they talk to us, do you think?"

"From time to time, yes, I think," Mrs Posnansky said. "But if you are not chosen, my dear . . . what will happen? You will be sad."

"I know. I try to get ready for not being chosen. I lie in bed and say to myself, Louisa, you are not going to be a mouse. You will be very sad, but it doesn't matter, because you will have tried your best, and there will be other chances."

"How sensible you are, Little Swan! I am admiring this very much," said Mrs Posnansky.

"But it's not true," I told her, and took another brandy snap.

"How, not true?"

"I *will* care, and I *will* be sad, and I won't even think for a minute about other times. I want to be chosen *this* time. I wouldn't tell anyone but you. And Annie."

Mrs Posnansky sighed. "The dancer's life is hard and filled with disappointment. This I know. Is hard that this sadness must begin when you are so young."

I munched in silence for a while, and then I said, "May I tell you something? I haven't told this to anyone else at all, not even to Annie. Do you promise not to tell anybody?

"Of course," said Mrs Posnansky. "You trust me."

"I'm going to be a bit disappointed even if I am a mouse. What I really want to be is a party child. Isn't that awful?"

"But why do you wish to be a party child?"

"Because the party children have a dance in the First Act and pretty clothes, and they get to be in the Land of Sweets as well. All the mice do is rush about in a great gang and they wear furry grey costumes that aren't a bit pretty. So that's what I'd really love, only that'll never happen, so I'm hoping to be a mouse. That's second best, but it's still good."

"I wish for you," said Mrs Posnansky. "Come and tell me the news. If it is bad, we take out the chocolate to cheer us up. If it is good we take out the chocolate to rejoice."

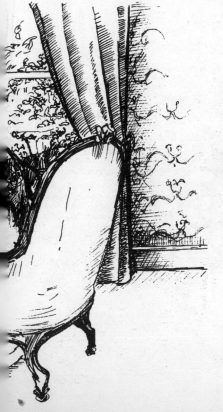

"You mean to celebrate," I said.

"Yes, yes," said Mrs Posnansky. "To celebrate."

On Saturday, the changing-room was very quiet. Nobody felt like talking. We all knew that today was going to be a very special lesson.

"I saw him," Eleanor said. "I saw Mr Sheridan arriving. He's in there with Miss Matting."

"How do you know it's him?" Emma asked.

"I've seen his picture in the paper," said Eleanor. "And he lookes just like a dancer. All in black with a walking stick."

We went into the hall, and there he was, just as Eleanor had described him. He was sitting very upright on a chair, and Miss Matting was standing next to him. He was very handsome, even though he looked quite old.

"Good morning, children," said Miss Matting. "This is Dominic Sheridan. I know you all know who he is. He's come to look at you this morning because he needs young dancers for *The Nutcracker*, and I'll let him tell you himself what he wants you to do."

Mr Sheridan stood up, and Miss Matting sat down.

"Greetings, children," he said. "I want you all to pretend that I'm not here."

We all looked puzzled. How could we possibly pretend that?

He went on. "I'm not going to ask you to do any special routines, or steps. I am simply going to watch you have your class as normal. I shall walk about and look at you more closely, and I just want to see you doing the things you always do. Now, I'm sure you all start with the barre exercises, so line up there and we'll begin."

All the time I was doing my barre

exercises, I felt cross. I'd been being a mouse all week for nothing. Now Mr Sheridan would never see how truly mouse-like I could be. I went through my pliés and demi-pliés, and out of the corner of my eye I could see Mr Sheridan looking at a piece of paper on a clipboard.

"I bet," whispered Phoebe, who was standing behind me, "that that's a list of our names. Can you see what Miss Matting is doing?"

I shook my head, no.

"I can," said Phoebe. "She's looking over here at us and then pointing. She's telling him what we're all called. That's what I think."

She sounded breathless and I could hardly hear her because she was whispering very quietly. When we turned round with our other hands on the barre, I was behind her, and I whispered to her:

"Are you nervous?" and she nodded her head, yes.

The class seemed to go on for ever. At last it was over.

"Thank you, children," said Mr Sheridan. "You are all a credit to Miss Matting. I'm sorry you can't all be in *The Nutcracker* but I do hope everyone will come and see the show, and support the people whom I have chosen. Let's see . . . . where is that list?"

Miss Matting gave him the clipboard, and he smiled at us. I was finding it very hard to breathe, and I could feel my face burning. I looked at Phoebe, and she smiled at me and held up her hand with the fingers crossed. How could she be so friendly at a time like this? Tony was staring out of the window and didn't even seem to be paying attention. How could he be so calm? Perhaps there was something wrong with me for caring so much.

"Mice first, I think," said Mr Sheridan. "Here we are: Tony Delaney, Colin Shand and Phoebe Winters."

I could feel myself wanting to cry. I'm not a mouse, I thought. They haven't chosen me. I'm not a mouse.

"And now, party children. Well, I'm afraid we only need a very few of these, so only one name here: Louisa Blair."

"Me?" I think I said. I can't really remember, because all of a sudden everyone was crowding round me, and Phoebe was hugging me. I remember that.

"Oh, Louisa," she said. "It's us! It's both of us! We're going to be in *The Nutcracker*. Really and truly! And Tony and Colin. Isn't it wonderful? It's the most delicious thing that's ever happened! Isn't it? Isn't it?"

I hugged Phoebe back. I couldn't help it, I was so happy. And I decided in that second, I liked her. I really did. There was nothing wrong with her. She was nice. And even though she didn't seem to know what 'delicious' meant, she was the only person who never, ever called me Weezer.

·······Chapter Four·······

All the rehearsals for *The Nutcracker* were being held in the studio which Mr Sheridan's company always used. This was at the back of a small theatre called The Playhouse, which was so far away from where we lived that Tony and I had to go on the bus.

"Are you sure," Mum asked the first time we had to go, "that you'll be all right? Will you know where to get off? And will you make sure you don't lose your fare money?"

I sighed. I was just about to moan at her for thinking we were babies, when Tony said, "Yes, we'll be fine, Mrs Blair. I'll look after Louisa."

"I can look after myself, thank you very much," I said and kicked him under the table. "Or maybe I'll have to look after you. You're always in a dream."

"I am not!" said Tony. "Anyway, we should go

or we're going to be late."

We weren't late. We'd set out so early that we were almost the very first people there. We waited for Phoebe to arrive. When she did, Tony and I waved at her, and after she'd got out of the car, she said, "Did you come by bus? That's silly. You must come with me in the car. We'll come and collect you next time. OK?"

"OK," I said. "Thanks, Phoebe."

"Yes, thanks," said Tony. "I'd love to ride in that car."

"Cripes!" said Phoebe. "This is it. Shall we go in?"

We went in, and a kind lady who was sitting knitting just inside the door said, "Hello, my darlings . . . you must be some of the mice, I expect. I think Mr Sheridan said you were to wait in the big rehearsal room. It's over there."

Other children began to arrive soon after. There were ten other mice, and a boy called Michael was my partner as a party child. Phoebe, Tony and I sat on a bench together. Dancers, real grown-up dancers, began to arrive, dressed in all sorts of strange things: torn sweatshirts, tatty leg-warmers, and ropey-looking scarves. The ladies all had huge shoulder bags, and their hair was scrunched up in ponytails. They didn't look in the least glamorous. One of them came up to us.

"Hi!" she said. "I'm Clara. I mean, my real name is Nikki, but I'm dancing Clara. Are you mice?"

"I'm not," I said. "I'm a party child. They're mice, though."

"It's going to be ever such fun," said Phoebe,

when Nikki had wandered away.

Mr Sheridan clapped his hands then, and we all had to go and stand in the middle of the room, while he explained what he wanted. Clara and the Nutcracker were going to dance first, and then we would do our bits. We sat on the bench and watched.

"He's not a bit like he was when he came to see us," Phoebe whispered. "He's shouting at them. Listen. Do you think he'll shout at us?"

Mr Sheridan *did* seem very cross.

"Nikki, darling, are you an elephant? Have you no idea of grace? What has happened to your arms? You are a young girl, not a shop-window dummy, sweetheart. Again, please."

"He says 'Again, please' so much . . . Do you think he'll be cross when it's our turn? I'm a bit scared," Phoebe said.

I was a little scared too, but I knew that famous choreographers often shouted at their dancers.

"He doesn't mean it," I said. "He just wants her to do her best. Anyway, I'm sure he won't shout so much at us. He hardly knows us."

When Clara and the Nutcracker came over to the bench, I could see that they were very sweaty. Nikki took a towel out of her bag.

"Your turn now, kids," she said to us. "He's a real slavedriver, but his bark is worse than his bite. Not much worse, but worse."

When it was the turn of the mice to do their steps, Mr Sheridan *did* yell at them.

"They're doing their best," I said to Nikki. "Why isn't he pleased with them?"

"Oh, Sherry never shows us when he's pleased. He reckons we only do well when we're terrified. Take no notice of him, that's my advice."

Tony and Phoebe looked a lot less terrified than the other mice. They went through the routine three times, and then it was the turn of the party children. We were going to do the scene in Act One, where everyone arrives for the Christmas party. There were four of us, and seven grown-ups.

"Michael and Louisa hold hands . . . Three skipping steps to the right, please . . . No, no, no, are you deaf, children? *Right*, not left. Really, what good are you to me as dancers if you don't know your right from your left?"

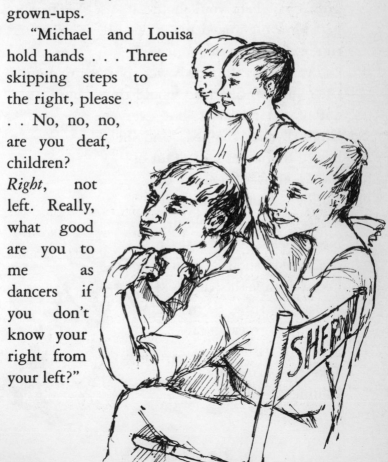

I couldn't help what happened next. I know you aren't meant to answer back, or argue during a ballet class, or a rehearsal. I know real dancers have to do exactly what they are told, but I lost my temper. Phoebe says I stamped my foot, but I can't remember that.

I do remember saying, "I *do* know my right from my left, Mr Sheridan, but it's hard to think properly when you shout at us. We're just getting a bit mixed up, that's all. It's the first time we've done this routine."

As soon as the words were out of my mouth, I felt sure Mr Sheridan would throw me out of the rehearsal, but everyone laughed and clapped, and he bowed to me and said, "Out of the mouths of babes, dear child . . . I am a brute and a beast, and apologize. Nevertheless, I shall continue to shout at you. I can't change the habit of a lifetime, I'm afraid. I mean no harm, I assure you. Take no notice of the volume of my remarks, just do what I tell you to, and all will be for the best. Now. Take Michael's hand, and skip to the right. Yes, like that. Good."

"And then," Phoebe said to Annie, "Louisa said, 'It's the first time we've ever done this dance,' and Mr Sheridan apologized. He actually apologized! Nobody could believe their ears."

We were sitting at the kitchen table in my

house. Phoebe's mother had given Tony and me a lift home, and arranged with our parents to pick us up and bring us back every time there was a rehearsal.

"That's extremely kind of you," my mother said. "Would Phoebe like to stay to tea? We'd love to have her."

"It's Friday, Mum," I said. "Could Phoebe stay the night? Then we can go to the Saturday class together tomorrow morning."

I said the words before I'd really thought, but as soon as our mums had agreed that it would be all right, and that yes, Phoebe could borrow some pyjamas, I felt really happy. I thought, I'll show her all my ballet stuff after tea. I couldn't wait for her to see my Little Swan headdress.

·······Chapter Five·······

"Being in *The Nutcracker*," Phoebe said to me as we watched Mr Sheridan shouting at the Sugar Plum Fairy, "is the most fun I've ever had."

I nodded. "I love these rehearsals. And next week we'll actually be in the theatre. We're trying on our costumes on Thursday."

Phoebe wrinkled her nose. "Yours will be nicer than mine. I'll be so hot in a mouse suit, and you'll probably have a lovely dress. I'm dead jealous."

One of the Snowflakes, the one Phoebe and I didn't like much, frowned at us. Whispering while the principals were working was not allowed. We pulled silly faces at her back when she turned away, but we *did* shut up. I thought about how strange it was that I liked Phoebe so much now. I'd tried to explain to Annie yesterday. Phoebe, I told her, was funny, and always let me look at her programme collection whenever I went round to see her. When I slept over at her house, she let me sleep on the top bunk even though I knew she liked it best. She never got bored with watching ballet videos, or talking about all the dancers.

But best of all, she really liked me. She told me all her secrets, and she said she enjoyed coming to our house because, as she put it, "You've got both the things I want most in the whole world: a sister and a cat. My mum says it's too late for a sister, and she's allergic to cats."

"I don't mind if you share Brad and Annie," I said, and we giggled. I hadn't said anything particularly funny, but that was just Phoebe. She giggled about all sorts of things. During *Nutcracker* rehearsals, Mr Sheridan called her Minnie, which I thought was a bit silly, but it made her laugh each time he said it. He called me Madam, and I didn't know whether he was being rude or polite, but he always smiled when he said it so I didn't mind too much. All the grown-ups made a fuss of us. Tony had more peppermints given to him than he could eat. The Nutcracker Prince shared his ginger biscuits with us, and the corps de ballet ladies let us listen to them while they gossiped. They also gave us nearly-finished lipsticks, and powder puffs they didn't like any more, so we started building up a make-up collection in a shoe-box.

A week before the first night, the snow fell.

"This makes everything really Christmassy," said Phoebe. "I love the snow."

"It's OK," I said, "but it turns to slush and then ice and you can't play snowballs any more. And it's cold. And it makes your gloves wet. And your shoes."

"Don't be a misery, Weezer," said Phoebe. Now that Phoebe came to our house so much and heard Annie calling me that, she'd started, and when I shouted at her, she didn't do what everyone else did and apologize at once. She said:

"You ought to be pleased that I'm calling you by your affectionate diminutive. It shows how much I like you."

"Affectionate *what*?"

"Diminutive. You know . . . like a pet name. Affectionate diminutive is what my dad says it is when he calls me Beebs."

"Beebs? That's worse than Weezer. Poor old you! Well, I shan't call you that."

"You can if you like. I don't care."

"Well, I care. I hate my whatever-it-was-you-called-it, so I'm not using yours."

One of the things Phoebe and I liked doing best

of all was watching the grown-ups rehearsing.

"I can do that bit," I said to her, as we watched the Sugar Plum Fairy from the wings. "Look at me!"

I started copying the steps. I'd been practising them at home and, apart from not being up on points, I thought I did it perfectly. Then I took a step sideways and stumbled. There were always pieces of furniture backstage and bits of the set as well. But I thought I knew exactly where they were. I forgot that a foot stool had just been put back after the party scene and I tripped over it in the middle of my dance. I clutched at a chair, but my feet just seemed to slip from under me, and I fell into a heap on the floor. My foot felt as if someone had bashed it very hard with a iron bar, and I started shrieking and crying, and all I could do was lie there. Everyone came running to see what all the noise was, and in the end I was sent home in a taxi with one of the ladies from the corps to keep me company.

"I want to go with her!" Phoebe cried. "Please let me go with Weezer. She's my friend." Even in the middle of my pain, this made me feel a bit better, but Mr Sheridan was rehearsing the mice, and didn't let her come. I looked out of the back

window of the taxi as it drove off, and there was Phoebe waving and weeping, wiping the tears away with the back of her hand.

The doctor came. Annie and my mum were just standing there looking worried while he poked and prodded at my foot. He arranged for me to go and have an X-ray, and then he bandaged it very tight, and told me not to walk on it.

"What about dancing?" I said. "I'm in *The Nutcracker*. At the Theatre Royal. It starts next week. Will I be OK next week?"

"Dancing?" The doctor shook his head. "You won't be dancing on this foot for at least three weeks."

"But . . . the show will be finished in three weeks! It's Christmas in three weeks. How can I just lie here while they're dancing in the theatre? What about my dance? I've got a dance with Michael. I'm in the Christmas party scene."

"Don't shout at the poor doctor, Louisa," my Mum said. "It's not his fault you've hurt your foot. I'm really so sorry, sweetheart. I know that dancing in *The Nutcracker* means a lot to you, but it would be silly to dance on that foot. You don't want to injure yourself in such a way that you couldn't dance when you were older, would you?

I'm dreadfully sorry."

I started howling, "Being sorry isn't any good! I don't care how sorry everyone is! I just want to dance. I'm never going to cheer up. Never. I don't care how hard you all try to make me feel better. I won't. So there. I shall feel miserable *forever*."

Annie looked so upset that I felt a bit sorry for her, but I was just too sad to say anything. This is the very worst thing that has ever happened to me, I said to myself, and it's all my fault. If only I'd been a bit more careful. It was horrible not to have someone else to be cross with. I wished I could just go to sleep and not have to talk to anyone. Brad was curled up next to me on the sofa and I picked him up and plonked him on my lap. I knew he wouldn't say anything.

Phoebe came to see me the next day. I was still sulking when she came in, but I stopped when I saw her. She looked as if she'd been crying for hours.

"Oh, Weezer," she said. "I've been crying for hours."

"I know you have. Your eyes are all red."

"I don't care. It's just so awful. It's the most awful thing I can think of!"

"You're the only one who thinks that. Apart from me of course. Everyone else tells me to cheer up and it could have been worse. They don't understand. You do. You know how I feel."

Phoebe started crying all over again. "I don't know how to tell you this, Weezer, so I'm just going to tell you. OK?"

Whatever did she mean? What was she going to tell me?

"Go on," I said. "What is it, Phoebe? What's the matter?"

"It's me. I'm the one Mr Sheridan has chosen. To do your dance with Michael in the party scene, and . . ." Phoebe could hardly speak she was crying so much. "The dress is beautiful. It's the most beautiful dress I've ever seen and you can't wear it. I feel so bad. I wish you could be in it. I do really. Do you believe me?"

"Of course I do," I said. I felt as if a huge stone was suddenly pressing on my stomach. I felt sick. I felt so jealous of Phoebe that I could hardly breathe, but she was crying so much, and she was so sad for me that I couldn't be cross with her.

"Don't cry, Phoebe," I said. "Really. I know that someone has to do my dance, and I'm glad it's you. Really. You'll be brilliant. I know you will."

Phoebe flung her arms around me and hugged me. "I won't be as good as you, Weezer. No one could ever be as good as you."

I started crying then, all over again. *That* was why Phoebe was such a good friend. She always seemed to say exactly the right thing.

········Chapter Six········

"You will come to the show, won't you, Weezer?" Phoebe asked. She had come to see me every day since my fall, and she'd told me all *The Nutcracker* news. "Everyone wants you to come, and Mr Sheridan says he told you you could have a box for the first night. You *must* come."

Everyone had been extra specially nice to me. The day after my fall, a huge bunch of flowers arrived and a card signed by every single member of the company. We didn't have enough vases, and we had to borrow from Tony's mum and from Mrs Posnansky. She brought chocolate, and a beautiful fluffy muff, made of something that looked just like proper fur. She told me all sorts of stories about her mother, and terrible things that had happened to her while she was a dancer.

"You remember, Little Swan, to learn from the bad things. This makes you strong."

• • • 53 • • •

"I don't mind not being strong," I said, "as long as I can dance. That's all I care about."

"But to dance you have to be very strong. Not just in the body, also in the head."

As the days went on, I did get a bit stronger in the head, but I was still sad. I didn't know whether going to see the show was going to make me feel better or worse. I was curious, though. I wanted to see Tony being a mouse, I wanted to see the dress I might have been wearing, and I *really* wanted to see how Phoebe danced my steps. I was getting very good with my crutches, too, and I'd been going to school every day in Tony's mum's car.

"OK," I said to Phoebe. "I will come."

"Brilliant!" said Phoebe. "My mum says she'll come and pick you up, and Annie and your mum, and Mrs Posnansky. The box is huge. Everyone will fit. And you must come backstage afterwards and see me. I told them you would. You will, won't you?"

"Oh, yes," I said. "I really miss everyone, even shouty old Mr Sheridan. I'm going to wear my best dress, and my new muff. I can't wait now."

"Nor me," said Phoebe. "Do you know, Mr Sheridan is always telling me how dreadful I am, and how unfortunate it was that that you fell over!"

"He doesn't mean it," I said. "He's just saying that."

But I couldn't help thinking about what Phoebe had said, and wondering if Mr Sheridan really *did* mean it.

I'd never sat in such a grand place to watch a ballet before. The seats were covered in red velvet and the curtains at the back of the box were also red, and matched the stage curtains. Mrs Posnansky had brought a fan in case we felt hot, and a pair of tiny little binoculars which she said were called opera glasses, even if you were watching ballet or a play. Annie and I had fun before the show started, looking at people in the stalls who didn't know we were watching them.

"Look at her hair," said Annie. "It's coming down at the back. Do you think she knows?"

"I can see Miss Matting over there!" I said when it was my turn to look through the glasses. "And Eleanor and her mother. If we wave, do you think they'll notice us?"

"You can't behave like that in a box," said Mum. "You have to be very lady-like in a box. And in any case, here's the orchestra. The lights will go down in a minute. Just sit quietly, please."

For once, I didn't mind doing what my mother told me to. I could imagine what Phoebe was feeling, backstage. I could imagine the butterflies in her stomach, and how dry her mouth must be. I listened to the music. Then the curtains parted and there was Fritz and Clara's house, and the Christmas tree in the corner, and there was Nikki, in a white dress with a blue pinafore, doing exactly the same steps I'd seen her do

Little Swan

many times, only because she was dancing under lights and in costume on a proper set, they didn't seem like steps any more, and then she stopped being Nikki, and became Clara. I heard my cue, the notes I always waited for before my entrance, and there she was, Phoebe, in a dress made of gorgeous, rustly, shiny taffeta, which was magic, because it looked green sometimes and red sometimes. It depended on whether the light was shining on it, or not. Phoebe and Michael did my dance, and I almost forgot that it *was* my dance. Phoebe did it beautifully. I felt happy and sad at the same time. I was happy for Phoebe, and sad for me.

In the interval, I tried to explain my feelings to Mrs Posnansky and Annie.

"I just wish it was me, that's all. I'll never know if I could have been as good as Phoebe, so I'm sad. But I'm happy that she's so good, because that makes the whole ballet good."

"This is natural," said Mrs Posnansky. "And your friend is good dancer, but she is not dancer like you. You have different style. She is quieter. She is more dignified. You are . . . you are lively. Sparkling. You are like quicksilver, she is like silk . . . slow and smooth."

I looked at Mrs Posnansky in amazement.

"That's what Phoebe said about my dancing. How did you know?"

"She said this? She is clever, then, as well as good dancer. I will come backstage with you to congratulate."

"Oh, yes," I said. "She'd love that. And I'm dying to see the rest of the ballet, aren't you?"

"Yes," said Mrs Posnansky. "Come, we will return to our box."

All four of us went backstage after the show. It took us a long time, because of my crutches, but I didn't mind. Half of me was still in the magical land where snowflakes danced, and Christmas presents came to life and took you to the Land of Sweets, home of the Sugar Plum Fairy who welcomed everyone to a place full of wonders, like flowers who could leap across the stage.

"Louisa!"

"Precious child!"

"Darling . . . you poor brave little thing, you!"

"Louisa, how divine to see you, pet!"

All sorts of people stopped us on the way to the big dressing-room where the mice and the children were changing. I hadn't thought that some of them even knew my name.

Mr Sheridan was standing in the corridor outside Nikki's dressing-room, and he bowed to me, and said, "My dear, I'm so sorry you had to miss this chance. Little Minnie Mouse did well, didn't she?"

"Yes," I said. "But I wish it could have been me. And thank you for sending those lovely flowers."

"We were all so sad for you, my little Madam! But you never know, there is always next year, isn't there?" He tapped the side of his nose with his finger, which was a very un-Sheridan-like thing to do.

"What do you think he meant?" I asked Annie.

"I think he'll let you do your dance next year."

"Really? You mean I'll get another chance?"

"I don't see why not. You said he puts on *Nutcracker* every year."

Suddenly, I felt perfectly happy. I went into the big dressing-room, where Phoebe and Tony were already in their own clothes.

"You were ever so good," I told him. "But you look funny. You've still got your whiskers on."

"They aren't whiskers," Tony said. "That's my mouse-tache. Ha ha!"

• • • 60 • • •

"That's a really pathetic joke, Tony," I said, but I giggled as well.

Phoebe ran over to me from the other side of the room. "Weezer! You're here! Hello, everyone!"

"You were lovely," I said. "You really, really were. And you looked great in my dress."

"It isn't your dress. It's *our* dress. You can have it another time."

"Yes," I said, "and we can both be famous at the same time. Mrs Posnansky explained to me that there are different kinds of dancers. She said we were like quicksilver and silk."

"Like Darcey Bussell and Viviana Durante."

"Exactly," I said. "We can do different parts. I'll do Coppélia."

"I'll do Giselle," Phoebe said.

"What about *Swan Lake*? I said. "I want to do that."

"So do I," said Phoebe. "Maybe we can take turns to do Odette and Odile. Louisa and Phoebe . . . Phoebe and Louisa. Doesn't that sound great, Weezer?"

"Yes, Pheezer. I think it sounds terrific."

"Pheezer?" Phoebe said. "What's that when it's at home?"

"It's your new affection-whatsit . . . dim-something."

Pheezer giggled. "I like it. Pheezer and Weezer."

"No," I said. "You've got it the wrong way round. Weezer and Pheezer."

Little Swan Ballet Books

*Louisa Ballerina's been bitten by the ballet bug!
There are four wonderful Red Fox books to collect
about Louisa and her ballet crazy friends.*

Book One - Little Swan

When Louisa's ballet class are going to put on a show
and do a dance from a real ballet in it, Louisa knows
there's only one place for her ... prima ballerina or bust!

£2.99 ISBN 0-09-921822-4

Book Two - Louisa's Secret

Louisa's new neighbour's great. There's only one problem
though - he's a boy, and boys and ballet don't mix!
But if anyone can convince him to give it a go,
it's got to be Louisa Ballerina!

£2.99 ISBN 0-09-921832-1

Book Three - Louisa in the Wings

When a famous Russian ballet company comes to town, Louisa just has to see them. Can she get the money for the tickets in time? Or is the show destined to go on without her?

£2.99 ISBN 0-09-921842-9

Book Four - Louisa and Phoebe

When new girl, Phoebe, arrives at ballet class, Louisa's nose is put right out of joint. She's nearly as good at ballet as Louisa is! But then, Louisa learns an important lesson. Just as good, doesn't necessarily mean just the same!

£2.99 ISBN 0-09-921852-6

Little Swan Ballet Books are the perfect read for budding ballerinas everywhere!